QUANTUM PHI

For Curious Kids!

This book belongs to.....

_____

First Published 2023
Copyright 2023
All rights reserved.

QUANTUM PHYSICS

for

Curious Kids

by Aidan Bettridge

For my own curious little kids

J, A and Q

A note from the author....

This book was originally written for my children. As a father of three curious and inquisitive children who love to ask why I wanted to help answer some of the questions they have about the world around them. A lot of us (myself included) find the entire concept of quantum physics difficult to understand because a number of the underlying principles are counter-intuitive to our everyday experiences. I believe exposing our children to these underlying principles of how the world works at the smallest scale while they are young puts them in an excellent position to build on this as they grow and learn. This book can be read together with your children of any age or independently by your elder kids. Happy learning!

TABLE OF CONTENTS

TABLE OF CONTENTS

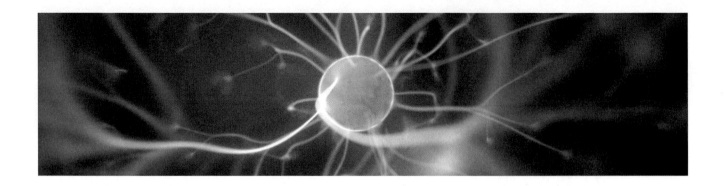

What is Quantum Physics?

Quantum physics is a branch of science that seeks to understand the behaviour of matter and energy at a very small scale. It deals with the fundamental building blocks of our universe, like atoms, particles and energy. Although quantum physics can be a complex and difficult topic to understand, it is also incredibly fascinating!

In this book, we will explore some of the basic concepts of quantum physics and try to explain them in a way that is easy to understand. By the end of the book, you will have a better understanding of the weird, wonderful and fascinating world of quantum physics!

The History of Quantum Physics

Quantum physics has an interesting history that started at the turn of the twentieth century. It began when a scientist named Max Planck discovered that energy comes in tiny packets called quanta. Then, Albert Einstein said that light is not just a waveform but can act like tiny particles called photons. Another scientist named Niels Bohr found out that electrons in atoms have specific energy levels and can jump between them by gaining or losing energy.

Then in 1926, Erwin Schrodinger came up with a special mathematical equation that describes how particles behaving like waves move. This equation has helped scientists understand how quantum systems work.

During this time, famous scientists like Einstein and Bohr had debates about how quantum physics relates to the real world. They argued about things like quantum entanglement, which is when particles are connected and interact even if they're far apart.

All these discoveries and debates led to the development of quantum physics, a new way of understanding the tiny world of particles and energy. Today, we use quantum physics in many exciting areas like electronics, computing, cryptography, and sensing.

So let's keep reading to learn more about the fascinating and sometimes counter-intuitive (i.e. it doesn't make sense) world of quantum physics!

Niels Bohr and Albert Einstein having a discussion in the 1920s. Quantum Theory was only in it's infancy!

Before we get stuck into the amazing and incredible world of quantum physics we need to understand a little bit about **matter and energy**. So let's find out what they are and how they act.

What is matter?

Matter is anything that takes up space and has mass. Everything around us, from the air we breathe to the ground we walk on, and the food we eat is made up of **matter**. But what is **matter** made of? Well, it is made up of tiny building blocks called atoms.

Atoms are incredibly small. So small that you can't see them with your eyes. To give you an idea of how small they are, imagine you are holding a tiny grain of sand. That grain of sand is made up of about 43 quintillion atoms (that is 43,000,000,000,000,000,000)!

Atoms are the basic building blocks of matter. They are like the letters of the alphabet that can be combined to make words, sentences, and paragraphs. Different types of atoms can be combined to make different types of matter, like the water in the ocean or the air we breathe.

The whole universe is made up of matter and energy. You, me, this book, the Earth, the sky, the stars and all the space in-between - it is all matter and energy! Quantum physics is the study of matter and energy at the smallest level.

What is an atom?

Atoms are the building blocks of everything, and in quantum physics, we explore how they behave. Atoms are made up of tiny particles called protons, neutrons and electrons. The neutrons and protons are in the middle (or nucleus) with the electrons spinning surrounding the nucleus, a bit like how planets orbit the sun.

The simplest atom is called Hydrogen. It is made up of one proton (in the nucleus) surrounded by one electron.

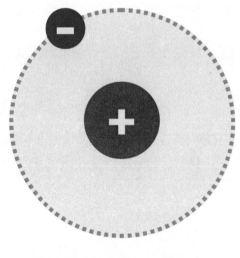

A hydrogen atom

The centre or nucleus of an atom is made up of positively charged protons and neutral (no charge) neutrons.

Electrons have a negative charge. They surround the nucleus of the atom moving in different 'orbits' depending on their energy level.

Atoms are made up of positively and negatively charged particles. Like the poles of a magnet, the positive and negative charged particles are attracted to each other

Atoms can swap and share electrons to create molecules. Molecules are groups of atoms that have joined together. This is how we get Chemistry!

What is energy?

Energy is what makes things happen. It is the thing that makes matter move and tells it where to go or what to do. Energy can take many different forms, like heat, light, and sound. For example when you put the kettle on to make a cup of tea the kettle uses energy to make the water hot.

There are two main types of energy:

1. Potential Energy

2. Kinetic Energy

Light, heat and sound are all forms of energy!

Potential and kenetic energy

Potential energy is the stored-up kind of energy that is waiting to be used. It's like winding up a toy car and putting it on the floor. The car has potential energy stored in its spring, but it's not moving yet.

Kinetic energy is the energy of things that are moving. When you let go of the toy car, it starts moving, and it has kinetic energy. So, things that are moving, like a ball rolling or a person running, have kinetic energy.

Before you let go of the car it has potential energy. After you let go and it's moving it has kinetic energy!

Energy and waves

Energy and **waves** are best friends. Waves are a disturbance that moves energy and can travel through different things, like air, water, string and even space! When waves move, they carry energy with them. Energy is the superpower that waves have. It helps them do amazing things! For example, light waves from the sun bring light and warmth to Earth. Waves in the ocean can push boats and surfers. So, whenever you see something moving like a wave, just remember that it's moving **energy** along with it. Waves and energy are a great team, always together and ready to make things happen!

Imagine a rain drop landing in a puddle. The drop of rain disturbs the surface of the puddle and gives it energy. This energy is transfered across the puddle by a small wave.

Quantum Energy

From a **Quantum Physics** perspective energy is the secret ingredient that tells the different particles how to behave. Particles can have different amounts of energy, which make them behave in different ways. Sometimes they move fast and sometimes they move slow, depending on how much energy they have.

In fact, energy is almost like a special kind of "money" that particles use to trade with each other. When they trade energy, they can change how they behave and even create new things!

But energy is not always predictable. Sometimes particles can borrow a little bit of energy for a short time, and then give it back. This means that energy is always moving and changing, and that's what makes our world so interesting!

Thanks for the energy!

Don't forget your change!

When particles collide they exchange energy. This can change how the particle behaves

Particles or Waves?

Now we know what **matter** and **energy** is we can move onto the tricky part. From the earlier pages we have come to understand that matter is made of particles and energy can be made of waves, but now I am going to tell you they can be both!

The duality principle of **quantum physics** is a little bit tricky to understand, but let me try to explain it in a simple way.

In the world of quantum physics, everything is made up of tiny particles that are so small that you can't see them with your eyes. These particles (like protons and electrons) can be like tiny little balls that bounce around, but they can also interact like wiggly waves that move up and down and transfer energy.

Should I be a particle or wave today? Maybe I'll just be both!

The Duality Principle

Now, here's the tricky part: sometimes, these particles can act like balls and sometimes they can act like waves, even though they are made of the same stuff! This is called the Duality Principle.

It's a bit like if you had a toy that could be both a ball and a bat at the same time. Depending on how you played with it, it would behave differently.

Scientists still don't completely understand why particles can act like both particles and waves, but it's an important part of how the world works on a really, really tiny scale.

One of the most famous experiments that shows how matter can act as both a particle (or a small ball) or a wave is the double-slit experiment.

The Double-Slit Experiment

The double-slit experiment is a really fascinating experiment that helps us understand how particles can sometimes act like waves.

Imagine you have a big wall with two tiny slits in it. You also have a special tool that can shoot tiny particles, like little balls, at the wall. When you shoot the particles at the wall, they go through the slits and hit another wall behind the first one.

Now, here's where things get interesting. If you shoot the particles one at a time, you might expect that they would hit the back wall in two straight lines, like you would see if you threw balls through the slits. But that's not what happens! Instead, the particles seem to create a pattern on the back wall that looks like the interface pattern created by waves.

Scientists think this happens because the particles are actually behaving like waves, not like balls. When the waves go through the two slits, they interfere with each other and create a pattern of light and dark spots on the back wall.

This experiment helps us understand that particles can behave in really strange and surprising ways, and that the world of quantum physics is full of mysteries that we're still trying to figure out.

The Double Slit xperiment with waves

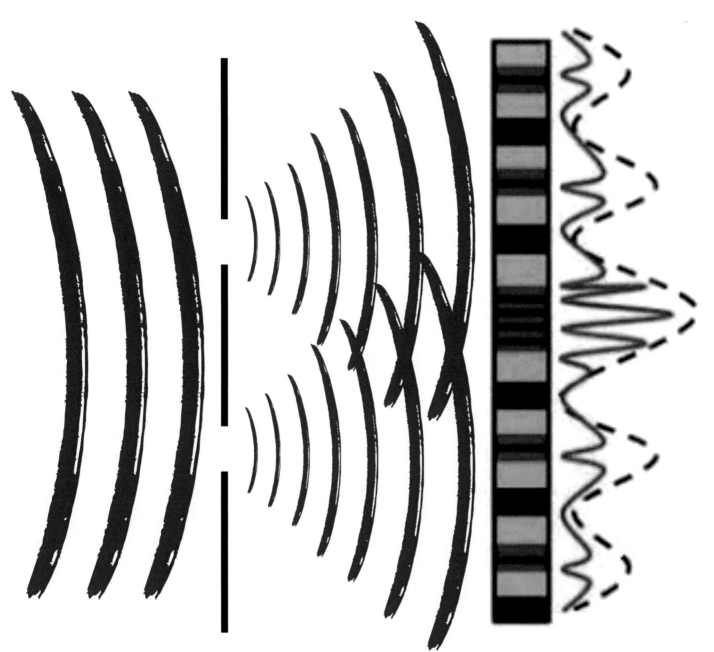

The waves split through the slit and then refract (a word we use in physics to describe how waves can bend) to rejoin and interfere with each other creating peaks and troughs.

The Double Slit Experiment with particles

Electron particles randomly shot at screen with two tiny slits

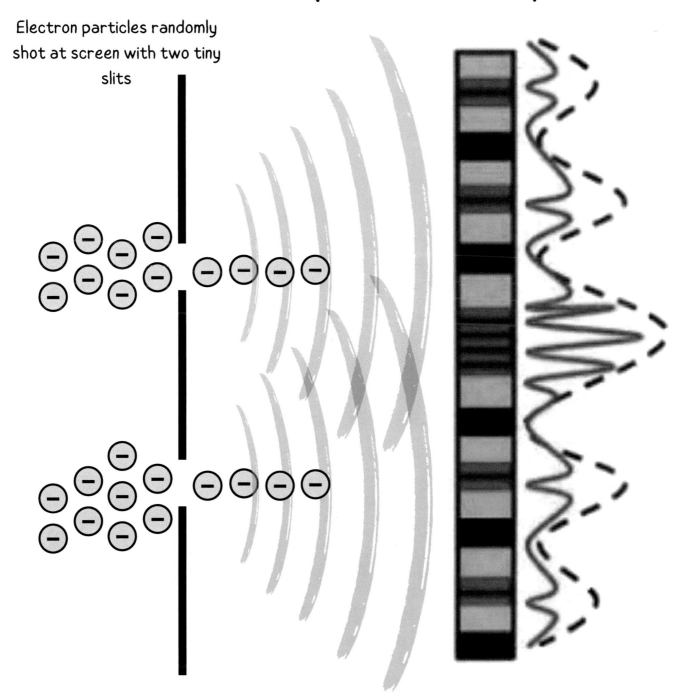

The particles interact and create a refraction pattern like they are waves. The pattern is similar to the one created by waves. This imples that the particles are behaving like waves with their position spread across a wave-function.

Light: Particle or wave... or both?

Let's take light for example. When we think of light, we often picture it as a wave, like ripples in a pond. Light is a transverse wave of electric and magnetic (electromagnetic) fields propagating perpendicular to the direction of the ray of light. The different wavelengths of light (the distance between the top of each wave) results in the properties of the light, like colour for example. But here's the twist: light can also act like a stream of tiny particles. These particles, called photons, zoom around and carry energy. It's like light is playing a game of hide–and–seek, switching between being a wave and being particles.

This duality of light has puzzled scientists for a long time. How can something be both a wave and particles at the same time? The truth is, we're not entirely sure. But this mystery has led to incredible discoveries and technologies. When light behaves like a wave, it can do things like bending around corners, creating beautiful colors, and forming interference patterns. We see this in magnifying glasses, rainbows and in the mesmerizing patterns created by sunlight passing through a prism.

On the other hand, when light acts like particles, it can explain things like how solar panels convert light into electricity and how cameras capture images. Photons are like little messengers of light, carrying energy and interacting with the world around them in surprising ways. But who first discovered that light could act like particles? It's time to meet Max Planck!

We get rainbows because light acts like a wave, but solar panels work because light acts like a particle

Plancks Quanta

Max Planck was a scientist who loved studying light and energy at the turn of the 20th century. One day, he was trying to figure out why heated objects, like a glowing piece of metal, emit light in certain colors. To solve this puzzle, he decided to investigate the nature of light itself.

As Max Planck looked more closely, he discovered something extraordinary. He discovered that light energy is not transmitted continuously like a flowing river (or like a continuous wave), but it comes in tiny, specific amounts called quanta. These quanta, or packets of light energy, came in discrete sizes.

These energy quanta, or packets, have fixed sizes, just like the pieces of a jigsaw puzzle. They cannot be divided or split any further. Max Planck called them "quanta" because it means "amount" in Latin. This is where the name quantum physics came from.

This discovery of quantisation revolutionised our understanding of how light and energy work. It helped scientists explain why heated objects emit specific colors of light and why certain substances can absorb only certain amounts of energy. For such an incredible discovery Max Planck won the Nobel Prize for Physics in 1918.

Quantisation showed us that the tiniest particles and energies in our universe behave in unique, discrete ways. It challenged our previous ideas that everything in the world could be smoothly divided infinitely. Instead, it revealed a whole new world of tiny, indivisible units. The Quantum world!

Max Planck won the Nobel Prize for Physics in 1918 for his discovery of Quantisation.

Wavefunctions and Superposition

Superposition is a peculiar feature of quantum mechanics. It means that a particle can simultaneously exist in multiple states or locations, as dictated by its wavefunction. It's as if the particle is spread out, exploring all possible paths or states at once. This is quite different from our classical intuition, where objects have well-defined properties and exist in a single state.

To understand this new quantum world new mathematical models were needed to help us understand how it worked. One of these models is called a wave function. Wavefunctions play a crucial role in describing the behavior of tiny particles, such as electrons. A wavefunction is a mathematical formula that captures important information about a particle's properties, like its position and momentum.

Think of a wavefunction as a mathematical way of describing the all possible locations of a particle. It's like a map that outlines all the places the particle could be in.

However, unlike our everyday experiences, where we only see things in one place at a time, in the quantum world, particles can exist in a superposition of states (that is they can be in lots of different places at the same time)! When we observe a particle, we "collapse" its wavefunction, which means we force it to assume a specific state or location. The act of measurement causes the particle to manifest as a definite entity in one particular state, and we see it in a specific position or with a specific momentum.

The wavefunction provides us with probabilities. Before we measure a particle, the wavefunction gives us the likelihood of finding the particle in different states or positions. The intensity of the wavefunction at a particular point corresponds to the probability of finding the particle there upon measurement. It's important to note that wavefunctions can evolve over time. They can spread out, contract, or change shape, guided by the laws of quantum mechanics. This evolution is often described by Schrodinger's equation, which governs how wavefunctions transform and influence the behavior of particles.

Schrodinger's Cat

In the wondrous world of quantum physics, there's a curious thought experiment (i.e. an imaginary experiment that only happens in your mind) known as Schrodinger's cat. It was created by the physicist Erwin Schrodinger to highlight the strange idea of superposition. Imagine a cat in a box with a mysterious device that may or may not release a deadly poison. According to quantum physics, until we open the box and observe the situation, the cat exists in a peculiar state of being both alive and dead simultaneously. This experiment was designed to question our understanding of reality and illustrate the bizarre nature of superposition and the challenges it poses to our intuitive understanding of the world.

Don't worry, Schrodinger never actually conducted this experiment. So no cats were hurt in the pursuit of physics! It is a thought experiment intended to help explain the concept of superposition.

The Uncertainty Principle

The uncertainty principle and Schrodinger's equation are both important ideas in a quantum physics.

The uncertainty principle says that when we try to measure something about a tiny particle, like its position or how fast it's moving, we can't know both things exactly at the same time. It's like trying to take a very clear picture of something very small — we can either know where it is or how fast it's moving, but not both perfectly.

Schrodinger's equation is a special math equation that helps us understand how these tiny particles behave. It's like a special rulebook that tells us how they move and change over time. It's really helpful because it helps us predict what these particles might do, even though we can't see them directly.

Spooky action at a distance

Quantum entanglement is an amazing phenomenon happening at the tiniest level of our universe! It was discovered by scientists named Albert Einstein, Boris Podolsky, and Nathan Rosen back in 1935.

Imagine you have two special particles, let's call them Particle A and Particle B. When these particles are entangled, it's as if they become best friends forever. They become connected in a very strange and unusual way.

After becoming entangled even if you separate Particle A and Particle B really far apart, they can still communicate with each other instantly! It's like they have a secret language that allows them to know what the other is doing, no matter the distance between them. Einstein called this phenomenon "spooky action at a distance" because it seemed so bizarre and incredible. He couldn't believe that particles could share information without any physical connection. It challenged our normal understanding of how things in the world work.

When scientists discovered quantum entanglement, they realized it had mind-boggling implications. It showed that the world of tiny particles doesn't follow the same rules as our everyday world. It's like a whole new kind of science is happening at the smallest scale.

Scientists are still trying to understand quantum entanglement better and use it to develop new technologies. It holds great potential for things like super-fast communication and super-powerful computers.

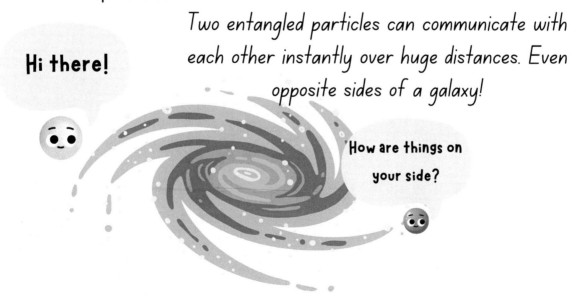

Hi there!

Two entangled particles can communicate with each other instantly over huge distances. Even opposite sides of a galaxy!

How are things on your side?

Schrodinger's Equation

Remember Schrodinger and his cat from a few pages ago? Well in the world of quantum physics, there is a special equation named after a brilliant scientist called Erwin Schrodinger. He discovered this equation in the year 1925, a long time ago!

Schrodinger's equation is like a secret formula that helps us understand how tiny particles, like electrons, move and behave. It's like a map that tells us where these particles might go and what they might do.

Imagine you have a little electron exploring its surroundings. Schrodinger's equation helps us predict where this electron might be at different times. It tells us how the electron's wavefunction, remember that special instruction manual we talked about earlier, changes over time.

The equation is full of complex mathematical symbols and calculations, but it's like a puzzle that scientists can solve to unlock the secrets of the quantum world. By solving this equation, scientists can figure out the probabilities of finding electrons in different places.

Schrodinger's equation has had a huge impact on quantum physics. It allows scientists to make predictions about how particles behave and interact with each other. It has helped us understand the strange phenomena of quantum mechanics, like superposition and quantum entanglement.

Thanks to Schrodinger's equation, we can develop amazing technologies like lasers, computer chips, and even quantum computers! It's like having a magical tool that helps us explore and harness the powers and mysteries of the quantum world

Quantum Physics in Everyday life

Quantum physics may seem like something that only scientists in labs study, but its influence actually extends beyond the realm of laboratories and into our daily routines. Here are a few examples of how quantum mechanics plays a role in our everyday lives:

1. Electronics: Quantum mechanics is at the heart of modern electronics. Devices like smartphones, computers, and televisions rely on transistors and integrated circuits, which make use of the behavior of electrons at the quantum level. Without quantum mechanics, these technologies wouldn't exist!

2. Lasers: Lasers are everywhere! They're used in barcode scanners, CD and DVD players, surgical procedures, and even in grocery store checkouts. Lasers work based on the principles of quantum mechanics, specifically the behavior of photons, which are tiny particles of light.

3. LED Lights: Light-emitting diodes (LEDs) have become popular in household lighting and electronic displays. Quantum mechanics helps explain how these efficient and long-lasting lights work. The quantum behavior of electrons in the materials used in LEDs allows them to emit light.

4. GPS and Atomic Clocks: The Global Positioning System (GPS) that you use in cars and on phones rely on atomic clocks, which are incredibly precise timekeeping devices. The accuracy of atomic clocks depends on the principles of quantum mechanics. Without quantum mechanics, GPS wouldn't be as accurate as it is today.

5. Magnetic Resonance Imaging (MRI): Quantum mechanics plays a crucial role in the technology behind MRI scanners, which are used for medical imaging. The behavior of atomic nuclei in strong magnetic fields, as described by quantum mechanics, allows doctors to see detailed images of our bodies without invasive procedures.

These examples just scratch the surface of how quantum mechanics impacts our daily lives. From modern communication technologies to advanced medical diagnostics, quantum mechanics has transformed the way we live and interact with the world.

So, even though the concepts of quantum mechanics can be mind-boggling, we owe many of our everyday conveniences and technological advancements to the amazing discoveries made in this field. Quantum mechanics is a hidden scientific superhero that quietly shapes our modern world!

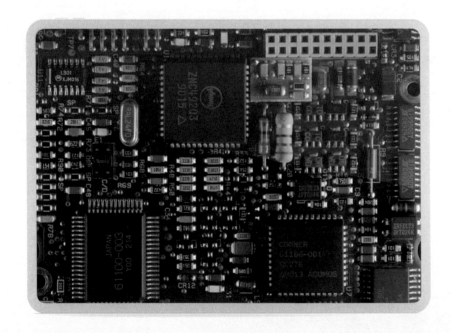

The future is Quantum

The field of quantum mechanics has already brought us incredible advancements, but hold onto your hats because the future looks even more mind—blowing! Scientists and researchers are exploring exciting possibilities that could revolutionise the way we live:

1. Quantum Computing: Imagine computers that can solve complex problems at lightning speed! Quantum computers have the potential to outperform traditional computers by using the unique properties of quantum mechanics. They could help us tackle complex calculations, optimize logistics, simulate chemical reactions, and revolutionize cryptography.

2. Secure Communication: Quantum mechanics could provide us with unbreakable codes and super-secure communication. Quantum cryptography uses the principles of quantum entanglement to create secure channels for transmitting sensitive information. It's like sending secret messages that no one can intercept or decode.

3. Quantum Sensors: Quantum mechanics offers the promise of incredibly precise sensors. These sensors could detect and measure things like magnetic fields, gravitational waves, and even individual molecules. This could lead to advances in medical diagnostics, environmental monitoring, and exploration of the universe.

4. Quantum Simulation: Quantum mechanics allows us to simulate and study complex systems that are difficult to understand or reproduce in the laboratory. This could help us develop new materials, optimize energy efficiency, and even understand biological processes at the molecular level.

5. Quantum Internet: Picture a super-fast, ultra-secure internet that connects the world like never before. The concept of a quantum internet is being explored, where information is transmitted using quantum bits (qubits) instead of traditional bits. It could enable secure communication, quantum computing collaboration, and open up new possibilities for global connectivity.

These are just a few glimpses into the potential future of quantum mechanics. The field is constantly evolving, and as we unravel the mysteries of the quantum world, we're bound to discover even more astonishing applications that could transform our lives.

So, get ready for a future where quantum mechanics takes center stage, powering technologies that were once only dreamed of. It's an exciting journey into a realm where the ordinary rules of physics are reshaped, unlocking a world of limitless possibilities!

Unified Theory of Everything

Hold on tight because we're about to dive into the ultimate quest of science — finding a grand unified theory that brings together quantum physics and Einstein's theory of relativity! These two incredible frameworks, despite their individual successes, currently don't fit together like puzzle pieces. Quantum mechanics explains the behavior of particles at the tiniest scales, while relativity unveils the secrets of gravity and the vastness of the cosmos. However, when scientists try to merge the two, they just don't fit. The mathematics and concepts of these theories clash, and they provide conflicting descriptions of reality. This mismatch is a fascinating puzzle that scientists are diligently working to solve, as finding a consistent framework that unifies these two powerful theories would be a major leap forward in our understanding of the universe.

Thank you for joining us on our adventure through the quantum world. If this has sparked your curiosity in science and the facinating quantum world there is so much more to learn. You could become one of the next great scientists to make the next big discovery and unlock the potential of quantum mechanics and the hidden secrets of our universe!

"Education is not the learning of facts, but the training of the mind to think."
Albert Einstein

QUANTUM PHYSICS

A world of (not quite)

infinite possibility!

Made in the USA
Las Vegas, NV
02 December 2023

81927200R00029